Pinkalicious®

Puptastic!

For Woof

The author gratefully acknowledges
the artistic and editorial contributions
of Daniel Griffo and Justine Fontes.

I Can Read Book® is a trademark of HarperCollins Publishers.

Pinkalicious: Puptastic!
Copyright © 2013 by Victoria Kann

PINKALICIOUS and all related logos and characters are trademarks of Victoria Kann. Used with permission.

Based on the HarperCollins book *Pinkalicious* written by
Victoria Kann and Elizabeth Kann, illustrated by Victoria Kann
All rights reserved. Printed in the United States of America.
No part of this book may be used or reproduced in any manner whatsoever without
written permission except in the case of brief quotations embodied in critical articles and reviews.
For information address HarperCollins Children's Books, a division of HarperCollins Publishers,
195 Broadway, New York, NY 10007.
www.icanread.com

Library of Congress catalog card number: 2012948580
ISBN 978-0-06-218786-4 (trade bdg.)—ISBN 978-0-06-218785-7 (pbk.)

15 16 17 18 PC/WOR 10 9 8 7 6 5 4 3
❖
First Edition

Pinkalicious®
Puptastic!

by Victoria Kann

HARPER

An Imprint of HarperCollinsPublishers

"I have news!" Mommy said.

"We are going to take care of a puppy.

The Razzles asked us to puppy-sit

Pinky this week when they are away."

Pinky and I will take long walks,
chase butterflies, and play fetch.

PINK PUPPY
PARK

"Taking care of Pinky will be pinkabulous!" I said happily.

"Pinky isn't really pink,"
said Daddy.
"She just has a pink nose."
"There's no such thing
as a pink dog," said Peter.

The next day, when the bell rang

I rushed to open the door.

"Hello, Pinky.

It's nice to meet you.

I am Pinkalicious!" I said.

Pinky didn't bark.

She didn't lick my hand.

When I tried to pet her, she hid!

12

"Pinky needs time to get used
to you," said Mrs. Razzle.
"I hope Pinky gets used to me soon.
I want to play with her!" I said.

"You have to get Pinky
to trust you," said Mommy.
"There must be something
I can do!" I said.

I tried to make friends.

Pinky just hid under the sofa.

She did not come out!

Pinky didn't come out for a ball.

She didn't come out to see her bed.

She didn't even come out

for a dog treat I made her!

"Try taking Pinky outside,"

said Mommy.

I picked up Pinky and carried her
to the backyard.
Everything scared her,
even butterflies.
Worst of all, Pinky was scared
of me!

We went back inside,
but I didn't give up.
I tried to see things from
Pinky's point of view.

Everything looks bigger

when you crawl

on the floor!

Poor Pinky had the blues!

The next day I got an idea.

"I know what I like to do

when I feel blue," I told Pinky.

Pinky watched me fill the tub.

Her tail wagged.

"You must like bubbles, too!" I said.

Pinky jumped into the tub!

She snapped at the bubbles.

Oops!

Mommy's bottle of Pink
spilled into the tub.
The water turned bright pink.

Pink bubbles splashed all over!

Pinky snapped at the bubbles.

Pinky was very happy!

When Pinky got out of the tub
she was pink!
Pinky looked at her paws.
Then she turned around fast
to see her tail.

Pinky looked puptastic!

She howled and I howled, too.

Pinky was so happy!
She let me pet her,
and she even let me put bows
in her fur.

I told my family what happened.

"Now there really is such a thing

as a pink dog!" I said.

Pinky licked Peter in the face.

"Ewww!" said Peter.

"I hope the Razzles like pink!"
Mommy said.

"Pinky is happy because she is now
as beautiful as her name!" I said.

28

The rest of the week went quickly.

Pinky and I took long walks

and played fetch.

We chased butterflies, too.

The Razzles were surprised to see

their puptastic dog.

Pinky is a pinkoodle now!

"I wonder if Pinky will stay pink,"

said Mr. Razzle.

I gave him a bar of green soap.

"Wash Pinky with this.

She will turn back to normal," I said.

I also gave the Razzles the ribbons.

"Pinky likes pink," I said.

"Maybe Pinky just likes you!"

said Mrs. Razzle.

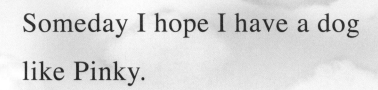

Someday I hope I have a dog
like Pinky.

For now, I'm just glad I helped
make her happy.